HOBO TOAD
AND THE MOTORCYCLE GANG

By Jane Yolen

Jane Yolen

Hobo Toad

and the Motorcycle Gang

Illustrated by Emily McCully

THE WORLD PUBLISHING COMPANY

NEW YORK AND CLEVELAND

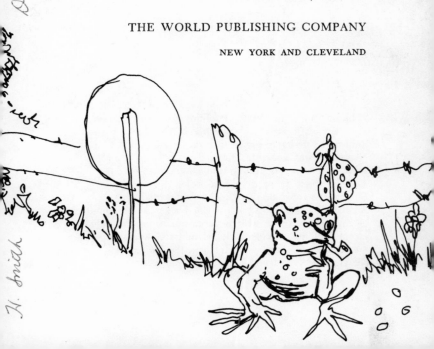

Published by The World Publishing Company
110 East 59th Street, New York, N. Y. 10022
Published simultaneously in Canada by
Nelson, Foster & Scott, Ltd.
Library of Congress catalog card number: 70-101843
Text copyright © 1970 by Jane Yolen
Illustrations copyright © 1970 by Emily McCully
Designed by Jack Jaget

To Elisa and Janey, who are loved

a big diesel truck with INFLAMMABLE on its side came roaring into view. It had almost passed by H.T.'s hitching thumb when it screeched to a lumbering halt. The door on H.T.'s side was swung open.

"Hop in, little fellow," called the truck driver, a burly man with a gold front tooth. He reached over and helped his passenger in.

"Thank you," said H.T. "Only I'm not so little. For a toad, that is."

"Well, well," said the truck driver, looking down at him, "so you're not. Looks are sometimes deceiving."

"That they are," replied H.T., who loved a good bit of philosophy.

"I mean," said the truck driver, "for instance, to

look at me, you'd never guess I was a poet, would you?"

"No. No, I wouldn't," said H.T. "I would guess you were a truck driver."

"Aha!" bellowed the driver. "And you'd be only half right!" He slapped his knee and laughed heartily. "But I'm Mac McNeill, though I prefer to be known as the 'Tennyson of the Truckers.'"

"As you said," said H.T., pulling out his acorn pipe and lighting it, "looks can be deceiving. Mind if I smoke?"

"Not at all, not at all," said Mac. "And do you mind if I sing you one of my poems?"

"A favor for a favor," said H.T. "The pleasure would be mine." He settled comfortably on top of his bindle and crossed his legs.

"A road song," said Mac, announcing his selection. He opened his huge mouth and started to sing:

> *"Oh, the joy of the open road,*
> *Running oooooooo-ver an occasional toad.*
> *Through—*

—oh dear," he added, "present company excepted, of course."

"I don't see why you couldn't have chosen a different animal," said H.T.

"But it rhymes," said Mac. "And besides, it happens, you know. Can't be helped."

"I'd rather not discuss it," said H.T. with dignity, and for a long while neither one said anything.

Presently Mac said, "You're right. It's just that I never knew any toads *personally* before. I thought they gave you warts." He looked over nervously at H.T. "You don't, do you?"

"Doesn't run in the family," said H.T. thoughtfully, puffing on his pipe. "Though I did hear of one great-great-aunt Matilda who had carbuncles."

"How's about I change the line?" said Mac. "It could go:

> *"Oh, the joy of the open road,*
> *Traveling with an occasional toad."*

"That's much better," said H.T. "Yes, I rather like that."

"Thank you," said Mac, relaxed now. "It's just that I'm taking poetic license with the *occasional* since this is really the very first *occasion* I've had."

"And I hope you have a great many more," said H.T. "Except, of course, you probably won't. Toads in general are rather stay-at-homes. You know, comfortable hole, warm and safe, food flying by within tongue's reach, that sort of thing."

"It must be a rather exceptional toad that travels," said Mac. There was admiration in his voice.

"Well, I won't say yes and I won't say no," said H.T. "Don't want to be made out a braggart."

9

"Wouldn't think of it," replied Mac.

And they turned and grinned at each other, a grin that said, "Isn't it grand when you meet someone who *understands*."

"Sing the rest of the song for me," said H.T.

And Mac did.

"Oh, the joy of the open road,
Traveling with an occasional toad.
Through the dawn and the dark and the dawn,
Traveling on and on and on and on and on.
Wheeling on down the dusty highway,
Picking up somebody going my way.
Oh, there's no joy like a big diesel load
But the joy, joy, joy of the open road."

When he finished, Mac sang it again and this time H.T. joined him in a tiny but robust voice. And when they got to the end, for the sheer joy of it, they sang it again.

"You have quite a voice for a toad," said Mac. "I would have expected more of a croak."

"You're thinking of frogs," said H.T., blowing a tiny ring of smoke into the cab.

"Am I?" asked Mac. "Well, maybe I am. I don't know much about the difference between them. Except the warts, of course."

"Which is an old wives' tale, I do believe," said H.T. A sudden bounce made him look out of the window nervously. "That wasn't—wasn't an occasional . . . ?"

"Just frost heaves," said Mac. "Happens this ti
of year. The frost makes the road buckle a bit a
bounces the truck around."

"Oh yes, I know about frost heaves," said H.T.
"Once got shoved out of bed by one. Thought it was
a troublesome mole. They're always taking wrong
turns and ending up in someone else's parlor. But
actually, a mole taking a *wrong* turn one spring did
me a *good* turn. Started me traveling, looking for a
new hole. I enjoyed the dirt under my feet and the
grass tickling my nose so much, I decided to keep on
the move all through the spring and summer. And
when fall came, I just hitched onto a freight and made
my way down to the Okefenokee. That's where I'm
heading now. Going to winter in the South again.
I've been traveling ever since that mole. Never regret-
ted a moment of it."

"What a life!" said Mac admiringly. "Now me, I
enjoy traveling. But just as a job. I want to be secure
—you know what I mean? I want to be sure I know
where the next meal is coming from."

"If you were a toad," said H.T., flicking his tongue
out and catching a fly that was buzzing about their
heads, "you *would* know."

"Aah, but I'm not."

"More's the pity," H.T. said with a sigh. "I think
you'd make an excellent toad."

"Thank you," said Mac.

"You're welcome, I'm sure," H.T. replied.

They drove in silence for a while.

11

At a railroad crossing, waiting for a slow train to pass, Mac turned suddenly to H.T. "By the way, you never did say your name," he said.

"Didn't I? By my mother's amber eyes, so I didn't. Well, it's H.T. Stands for—"

"Let me guess," boomed out Mac. "Hop Toad."

"You've been peeking at my passport," said H.T., just a little crossly.

"No, no," Mac said quickly. "But I'm right, aren't I?"

"Not quite. It's Hopalong Toad, though I'm now mostly called Hobo Toad or H.T. for short. My mother, bless her jeweled head, was in love with a movie cowboy. Said his eyes were as big and as beautiful as a toad's. She saw his picture on a magazine someone had thrown away and she used it as a bedspread. Made my father so furious, he was about to leave home when a flash flood washed away picture and hole and all. I was born in a damp, dark cellar and Mother named me Hopalong in memory of that cover."

"Beautiful. Beautiful," said Mac. "It almost makes me cry."

"I think you'd better shift gears instead," said H.T. "The train has passed and the barrier is up. And I hear some angry honking behind us."

Mac threw the big truck into gear. It growled and grumbled and then slowly bumped over the tracks. In a moment, the two travelers in their truck were speeding along the highway again, bound for the South.

the truck hurtled down the highway toward Florida. Inside the cab, the big driver and the little toad were lost in thought, their heads wreathed in acorn pipe smoke.

As they rounded a bend in the road, an enormous sign flashed on top of a hill.

The sign, which was bright red, said GREAT KATE.

Before either the toad or the man had time to comment on it, they rounded another curve in the road and saw another flashing sign. This one was in blue. It beamed KATE'S GRATE.

"Hmmm," Hobo Toad ventured. But before Mac could reply, they had gone around another bend and a third sign read in yellow KATE'S GREAT.

13

Then suddenly, rounding yet another curve in the road, they saw a simply enormous sign flashing in all colors of the rainbow GREAT KATE'S GRATE. IT'S GREAT. SO'S KATE. Underneath was a small dilapidated trolley car that had been renovated into a small dilapidated diner. There was a sign on the door that said in very small letters: *This Is It!*

"It pays to advertise," said H.T. cryptically.

"I've heard of Great Kate. They say she makes the best pies between Boston and Florida, but I've never tried any. I'm hungry. Let's stop."

"Pies mean flies," said H.T. "I wouldn't say no."

Mac slammed on the brakes and the enormous truck came to a shrieking, shuddering halt.

"Shouldn't you be a little more careful?" asked H.T. "After all, it does say 'flammable' on your truck."

"Nope," Mac answered. "Says 'inflammable.'"

"Same thing," said H.T. "Both mean it sets on fire easily."

"I know," said Mac. "But it's not true. I mean, about what I carry."

"Oh?"

"It's a load of marbles, actually," said Mac. "I work for the Greater Boston Marble Company. Their motto is *If You've Lost Your Marbles, We'll Replace Them.* They got the truck at half-price at a fire sale, and they left the original sign, 'inflammable,' right on it. The president felt that a huge truck with 'marbles' written on it would look silly."

14

And with that explanation, Mac opened his door and went around to the other side and opened the door for H.T. Then the two went into Great Kate's Grate.

Behind the counter stood Kate. It was easy to see how she got her name. She was the largest woman that H.T. and Mac had ever seen. Her dress was covered with buttons and seemed ready to burst in all

15

directions. In fact, it seemed as though the dress was holding all of Kate together, and the buttons were holding the dress.

"If one button goes," whispered Mac to H.T., "there goes the whole shebang. We'd have to duck. She'd explode like a machine gun."

H.T. put his hand to his heart in mock horror. "Cut down in my prime," he sighed. "By a round of buttons."

The two friends laughed and sat down.

Kate, who had overheard the whole exchange, laughed with them. "Don't worry," she said. Her voice boomed. It was as big as the rest of her. "Ain't lost a customer yet!"

She made a pass at the counter with a damp cloth. "But people come for miles just to see if I still have all my buttons."

"I hear they come to eat your pies," said Mac.

"Come to see my buttons," said Kate, "and stay to eat my pies. What'll you have, boys?"

"What have you got?" asked Mac.

Kate gestured to the wall in front of the counter. It had writing all over it. It read:

PIES   ONE SIZE

Apple	Peach	Rhubarb	Succotash
Banana	Plum	Apricot	Tangerine
Onion	Pear	Orange	Cauliflower
Cherry	Strawberry	Gooseberry	Blueberry

16

Mince   Carrot
Prune   Grape
Pumpkin   Chicken
Cranberry   Fish

Raisin
Spinach
Boston Cream

OR ANYTHING ELSE YOU WISH

Today's Special

"Wow!" exclaimed Mac. "A poem in twenty-seven flavors! How will I ever choose?"

"Of course, there's always Today's Special," said Kate. "One of my Surprise Pies."

"What are those?" asked Mac.

"You never know. There's always something surprising in them. I don't even know myself."

"Sounds great, Kate. I'll have one of them."

Kate leaned on the counter and looked at H.T., who had jumped onto the Formica top. "And what will you have, little fellow?"

"I'll just catch something on the fly," he said, winking one of his amber eyes at Kate.

Kate threw her big head back and began to laugh. The hundreds of buttons on her dress jiggled and twinkled. "Be my guest!" she said when she finished laughing. "Won't even charge you! Where there's pies there's flies!"

Spinach
Boston Cream
ELSE YOU WISH
'S SPECIAL

"My sentiments exactly," said H.T., and his tongue flicked out and expertly caught a fruit fly. He moved back to the comfortable stool.

"Prehensile," said a sinister voice from behind them. "To all intents and purposes, prehensile. Your tongue, sir."

H.T. and Mac turned around, but they could not see anything at all.

"What the—" said Mac.

Kate's face was suddenly very sober. Even the buttons on her dress stopped twinkling. "It's the Professor," she said. "He's back in town. I knew his leaving was too good to be true. He must have sneaked in when I was in the kitchen. He's always sneaking, that one."

"Evening, gentlemen," said the sinister voice without a body. Then suddenly a forehead appeared above one of the booths. Then more forehead. And more. Then two very small eyes and a face. "I am the Professor," said the head. It looked like a very large, lopsided, unshelled peanut. What made it especially queer, besides the great dome of a forehead, was the fact that it had absolutely no hair. No eyebrows. No eyelashes. No hair at all. But there was a smile. A sinister smile. An ugly smile. An absolutely evil smile.

"And you, sir, must be the driver of that very large truck marked 'inflammable.' How nice. How nice. And how convenient."

"What do you mean—convenient?" asked Mac. He positively growled. He didn't like the Professor at all.

"You'll find out," said the Professor. "You'll *all* find out," he purred. It was like a cat purring before pouncing. "Yes, you will all find out. In time."

Like some oily substance escaping through a crack, the Professor oozed out of the door and was gone.

Kate reached under the counter and got out a spray can of air freshener. She whisk-whisked at the door and the booth for well over a minute before she was satisfied.

"Flies are clean compared to him," she said to H.T. and Mac.

"I never thought flies were dirty," commented H.T. to no one in particular.

Kate leaned her huge arms on the counter. "I'll tell you something about him. Every time he shows up, there's trouble in this town. Last time he appeared, the mayor's house was robbed. Time before that, the museum burned down. And the first time he passed through, we had a blackout for three days. Nobody's ever proved anything, but when he's around—things happen."

"Maybe he's like a magnet," said Mac. "Attracts evil."

H.T. flicked in another fly. His sides twitched as the fly gave one last struggle in his stomach. "No, I think it's more than that. He seemed to me to like to make bad things happen."

Kate stood up. "I think you're right, little fellow. I think you are *absolutely* right." She turned toward the kitchen, smoothing down her dress and setting

the buttons to twinkling again. "And don't think I've forgotten your pie. One Surprise Pie coming up!"

She came back in a minute with a steaming pie that had three teardrops cut in the center. First wiping the counter in front of Mac, she placed the pie on the clean wet spot. Then she found a plate and a knife and fork under the counter and put them next to the pie. At last she pulled out a napkin that looked as though it had been sewn for someone her own size. Since Mac was just as big as Kate, that was fine.

Mac sniffed the air, first with his eyes open, then

with his eyes closed. He took a forkful of pie and chewed it slowly, savoring it. With his mouth still slightly full, he said, "I feel a song coming on. May I?"

Kate stood with her hands on her hips. "I'd feel complimented," she said.

H.T. took out his pipe and lit it. "Sing on, McNeill," he said, smoke beginning to curl about his head.

And Mac sang:

> "*I sing of pies of tremendous size,*
> *Of twenty-seven flavors,*
> *I sing of pies of some surprise*
> *And some surprising favors.*
> *I sing of pies and realize*
> *The hunger this engenders,*
> *So it's no surprise when this king of pies*
> *Contains . . .*"

At this, Mac dug into the middle of the Surprise Pie with his fork and pulled out a long soggy pair of

> "*. . . red suspenders?*"

"That *is* a surprise," said H.T. "Hardly edible, but certainly a surprise."

"I was going to say," Mac said, rather downcast, "*Contains surprising splendors.* But I suppose *suspenders* rhymes just as well."

"Oh dear," said Kate. "It's that Professor. I knew it!"

"Isn't this the surprise?" asked Mac.

"Oh, it's a surprise, all right," said Kate. "But hardly the one I had planned. My Surprise Pies have candies or edible favors in them."

"But never, I take it, red suspenders," said H.T., blowing a smoke square.

"Certainly not," said Kate. "But the interesting thing is that red suspenders—thirteen pairs of them— were missing yesterday from Bedelkamp's General Store."

"Now, that *is* peculiar," said Mac.

"But that's not all," said Kate. "Before that, three cans of red paint and one can of black were gone from Warter's Paintery. And three lengths of hose but only one nozzle were snatched from Dreedle's Hardware. A collapsible ladder disappeared from Spencer's Carpentry Shop. A spotted dog was lost from the K-Nine Kennel. The elementary-school bell was taken from the tower. And it all started last week when a pickup truck was missing from Larry's Auto Repair."

"Put them all together and they spell—" said Mac.

At that very moment, a fantastic squealing and screeching was heard outside: a rumbling and growling and racing of engines. The door was thrown open and a gang of twelve black-leather-jacketed motor-cyclists stamped, stomped, stumbled, and strode into the diner.

"—trouble," said H.T.

"**P**ies!" shouted the ugliest brute, who was obviously the leader of the pack. He was over six feet tall with a big black bushy moustache. On the back of his jacket was a picture of a horned devil with fangs dripping blood. On each arm the words "Baal" and "Beelzebub" and "Satan" were written over and over in red paint. His boots clanked as he walked for there were wicked-looking spurs attached to the heels. And he glowered. It was his best expression. Indeed, it was his only expression.

"Pies!" the leader shouted again. "And I want apple!"

"Cherry."

"Orange."

"Banana."

"Peach."

"Plum."

"Rhubarb."

"Strawberry."

"Blueberry."

"Spinach."

"Gooseberry."

"Banana Cream."

As each one of the leather-jacketed thugs sat down at the counter, he pounded his fist on the table and called out the name of the pie he wanted.

Suddenly the door was tugged open. A skinny, bespectacled boy with a black leather jacket started in. He tripped over the doorsill and grabbed the back of a booth to right himself. But when he tried to stand, he found that his spurs were stuck fast in the door which had slammed shut behind him. He yanked his feet away, leaving the spurs caught in the door. Then he strode over to the counter, trying to look nonchalant, and sat down.

"Pies!" shouted the head of the gang, who was known as Glorious Leader. "I want apple!"

The others, who had such names as Meatball, Risky Rob, The Hair, Slop, Bobordick (who were twins with the same name) and Ultimate Cool, shouted their orders, too.

"Cherry."

"Orange."

"Banana."

"Peach."

"Plum."

"Rhubarb."

"Strawberry."

"Blueberry."

"Spinach."

"Gooseberry."

"Banana Cream."

All twelve of the leather-jacketed hoods turned to glare at the boy, who hadn't ordered yet.

"Chicken!" he squeaked at last.

"CHICKEN?" they roared.

"No one in the Devil's Dozen orders chicken!" thundered Glorious Leader. "We don't believe in the word."

"But," squeaked the boy, and his glasses started to fog up, "I *like* chicken pie."

"HE LIKES CHICKEN PIE!" shouted Glorious Leader.

There was a sudden hush while the dozen motor-cyclists considered this possibility. Then Glorious Leader leaned over Bobordick and Slop and picked the boy up by the front of his leather jacket. "If you wasn't the Professor's son . . ." he said.

"*Adopted* son," squeaked the boy.

"Arrrrrrgh," said the leader and dropped the boy where he sat. Then he banged his fist on the counter again. "PIES!" he shouted.

In order to keep the gang from going through their

litany again, Kate ran into the kitchen and came back with the pies, six at a time, three balanced on each arm. She set them down in front of the hoods who did not even wait for napkins or plates. Then she went back for the next six. As she started back for the third time, to get the boy's chicken pie, she heard a wild shout. It was H.T. "Duck!" he cried.

Without thinking, Kate ducked. H.T. threw himself under the counter. And Mac hid behind a booth.

Each of the gang members had picked up his pie. Shouting and laughing, each one of the Devil's Dozen had thrown his pie right into the face of his neighbor, calling out, "PIES IN THE EYES! SURPRISE!"

Then they fell off their stools laughing and pommeling one another on the backs, and wiping the pie from their faces with grease-stained handkerchiefs. Only Kate, Mac, and H.T., who had ducked, and the boy who had remained pieless, were spared.

The door opened silently and a strange figure slithered in. "Gentlemen, to business. Amusement time is over."

The Professor had returned.

Immediately the motorcyclists got to their feet, pie running down their moustaches and beards, dripping onto leather jackets, sliding and sloshing onto Kate's once-clean floor. They tucked their grease-stained handkerchiefs back into the pockets of their dungarees and climbed back onto the stools at the counter.

"First," said the Professor, "another round of pies.

rhubarb
blueberry
cherry
apple
butterscotch
raspberry
apricot

To be *eaten* this time. Energy, you know. Stimulate the gray cells."

Kate shook her head as she surveyed the mess. "Out! I want all of you out of here."

The Professor snapped his fingers. Two of the gang leaped over the counter and sat Kate down hard on a stool while the Professor's adopted son, whose name was Samson, went slowly into the kitchen and got the pies.

"Get your hands off me," shouted Kate, her buttons jiggling angrily. But the two thugs tied her hands behind her and put a napkin around her mouth for a gag. The twins, Bobordick, grabbed Mac and tied him to one of the counter stools. Then one thug, named Creep, a redhead with hair down to his shoulders, tied H.T. to a large salt shaker, and started to shake them both.

"He'll give you warts," said Mac. Creep, who was proud of his hair and skin, backed away quickly.

"Thanks," said H.T., staring down at his pipe, which had been smashed to bits in the struggle. His gold-rimmed eyes were almost expressionless.

Mac nodded. He tried to twist his hands free but the knots held tight. "Made by experts," he said glumly. And with that, H.T. had to agree.

Through all this, the boy Samson had looked quite sad. He seemed somehow removed from all the goings-on. He just sat quietly at the counter eating his chicken pie and refusing to meet anyone's eyes.

"We are lucky, gentlemen," said the Professor, smiling his evil smile. "We have been given a present in the form of a truck with inflammable contents. It was to get such a truck that I chose Great Kate's Grate as our headquarters, since trucks stop here all the time. But I didn't expect to catch one this soon. Still, since we have everything else we need, we can start tomorrow. And now, gentlemen, I will tell you all my plan."

the Professor climbed onto the counter so that he could be the center of attention. He was dressed in a very fine herringbone tweed suit and a matching tweed tie. But he wore sneakers on his feet. His body, short in comparison to his enormous, elongated, hairless head with its great domed forehead, seemed to have a mind of its own. It twitched and scratched and settled at last into a cross-legged position on the Formica countertop. The head seemed to balance precariously on the scrawny neck. Yet for all the awkwardness with which he seemed put together, the Professor could move with an oily grace.

Around the Professor, on the stools, hunched the

twelve members of the Devil's Dozen. The thirteenth black jacket, the skinny Samson, huddled miserably around his chicken pie, shoveling it spoonful by spoonful into his mouth. ("Poor child," thought Kate, "they don't feed him.")

H.T. and Mac, trussed up like Christmas turkeys, had been thrown together in a heap on the floor behind the counter. Kate was shoved there with them, the gag still tight in her mouth.

The Professor had pulled down all the shades on the diner's windows and put an OUT TO LUNCH sign on the door though it was already well past dinnertime. He didn't want to be disturbed while he expounded his wicked plan.

"Gentlemen, you may wonder why I have called you here together," he began in his best after-dinner voice. He was used to lecturing, having been a popular woman's club speaker for many years despite his evil appearance. Indeed, the clubwomen seemed to like him better for it. His subject had been "Wild Flowers I Have Known." Of course, he had never let the Devil's Dozen know this. And indeed, it had been so long ago that the Professor had convinced himself that his years had been spent lecturing on "Amanita, Deadly Nightshade, and Other Poisonous Growths." He had told himself this lie so often, he now believed it.

As the Professor began, the slumping black-jacketed crew grew more round-shouldered as they bent forward to hear him. The Professor was such a spell-binder that Samson poised in mid-spoon to listen. And even H.T., Kate, and Mac strained in their bonds.

"Gentlemen, we are about to execute the crime of the century, the crowning achievement of my life."

"Aaaah," said Glorious Leader.

"Ah-haaaah," echoed his troop.

"Tomorrow we are going to rob the First National Bank of Secundo which will be overflowing with factory payrolls. We are going to do it with the help of our truck driver friend here. And in broad daylight, too!"

Mac jumped to his feet, even though his hands were still tied behind him. "I am not your friend," he shouted. "And I am *not* going to help you!"

The Professor snapped his fingers. Bobordick, both of them, leaped over the counter and sat on Mac. "And now to my plan. My beautiful plan."

"Does it use the thirteen red suspenders?" asked Meatball.

"And the paint?" asked The Hair, who had a long pigtail.

"Yes. And the hose and nozzle and ladder and truck, not to mention the spotted dog and the school bell," said the Professor.

The heads on top of the leather jackets all nodded and fingers snapped.

Kate said, "Mmmmmm, mmmmmm, mmmmm!"

which meant "I knew he had something to do with all that missing stuff," but was the best she could do under the circumstances. The circumstances she was under, of course, were the napkin gag.

"You tell us, Prof!" called out Glorious Leader.

"Yeh!" That was The Hair.

"Zap it to us!" said Meatball.

"Let us have it!" called out Slop.

Each one of the Devil's Dozen had something encouraging to call out.

"It is a simple plan. But foolproof. Foolproof!" said the Professor, smiling to himself. "That's why I picked such fools to execute it."

The thugs smiled and nodded. They thought it was a big compliment.

"When we finish, I will be recognized as the world's greatest criminal mind. No mean feat, I might add. Competition from government and universities has been great lately."

"Yeh!"

"Tomorrow," continued the Professor, "we will load Great Kate here and her two friends into the truck with inflammable contents that is parked outside. We will first, of course, fix the brakes. Fix them, that is, so that they will *not* work."

"Ha, ha, ha," laughed the hoods.

"Then I will send it and its inflammable contents down the big hill into Secundo because at the bottom of that big hill is—"

"THE FIRST NATIONAL BANK OF SECUN-DO," shouted the Devil's Dozen, slapping each other on the back and bopping one another's heads and pulling ears, and playfully tweaking noses till they were black and blue and occasionally green and purple.

"Correct," said the Professor. "And where will you all be all the while?"

"Where?" the hoods asked in awe.

"At the bottom of the hill around the corner from the bank."

"?" said the gang. The question was so loud, it could almost be heard.

"Ah, yes, that is the *real* beauty of the plan. You will be around the corner from the bank, my friends, in the pickup truck newly painted with the stolen paint, with the long hose fitted with a single nozzle, with the aluminum ladder, and the spotted dog on the running board and the school bell on top of the cab. And you will *all* be wearing red suspenders. Even you, my dear Samson. Because, my friends, you will be the new Secundo Volunteer Fire Brigade going to rescue all that lovely money from the flames!"

"Wow!" shouted Glorious Leader. "Brains!"

"Wahoo!" shouted the hoods, jumping off their stools and rushing to touch the Professor's feet because they thought that was where brains were to be found, their teachers always having told them that's where theirs were.

"You see, my friends," shouted the Professor, his voice rising to overcome the pandemonium, "no one, not even the local police themselves, will stop you because you will be firemen performing your *duty*. And if there is one thing people respect as much as they hate, it is *duty*!"

"Hurray for the Professor!" shouted the thugs. And "Two-and-a-half cheers for the Prof and one-half for our Glorious Leader." And they shouted and threw their motorcycle hats and goggles into the air. These landed on their heads, and Slop, who had a soft spot on his skull, was knocked out for a minute. And when

he regained consciousness, he shouted louder than anyone else.

"But, Father," came a squeaky voice from the corner. It was Samson. "What will happen to Miss Kate and the big truck driver and the little toad?"

"Why, what do you think will happen to them?" asked the Professor with a leer.

"They'll be burned up," said the boy in a very small voice.

"Correct," said the Professor. "You will make a professor yet."

"Oh," said Samson and he pushed the pie away. He was suddenly very full of chicken.

it was dark out as well as in. Glorious Leader had checked by peeking under one of the drawn curtains before he turned off the diner's light. The other hoods, collapsed on tables and slumped in the booths, were snoring away the tens of pies they had consumed to celebrate the Professor's plan. Even the Professor was asleep in the kitchen on Kate's enormous cot, his knees tucked under his chin, like an ugly, evil baby.

The diner was like a bomb—deadly, black, with the steady drone of the snores ticking away the minutes before it would explode.

Only H.T., Mac, and Kate were awake. Fear was in Kate's enormous eyes; anger in Mac's. And the toad swelled with rage, puffing and unpuffing his body as impossible plans raced through his wide-awake mind like dreams.

Suddenly a movement in the dark startled them. Involuntarily, they leaned closer to one another as though touching would protect them. Something scraped closer and closer to where they huddled, bound and helpless.

"Mmmmmmm?" asked Kate against her gag.

"I don't know," Mac whispered. "But don't worry." He knew he couldn't help, but Kate relaxed as though he could.

"It can't be any worse than what we're into now," added H.T., numbly wishing he had his pipe to suck on. It helped him think.

"*Psssst*," came a whisper. A squeaky kind of whisper. "It's me—Samson."

"Samson!" they all breathed.

"I couldn't let them do it to you," he said in a hushed voice. "I mean, motorcycles and leather jackets and blood oaths and that sort of thing are okay. It's just for show. But I never really thought they meant anything by it. And my father, my *adopted* father, he talks about things all the time. But I though it was just talk. Not really bad, you know. Not really—"

"Evil," said H.T.

"Yes," said Samson. "He always has this saying, you know. *Evil spelled backwards is live*. He had it engraved on his calling cards. I thought it was just silly talk. Make believe. But it's not—is it?"

42

"No," said Mac.

"So I thought I'd better let you all go, and take the consequences," said Samson.

"Thank you," Mac said.

Samson untied Kate's gag first. "I'm sorry Miss Kate. That must have been uncomfortable."

"Haven't been quiet that long since I learned to talk," said Kate. She smiled at the boy. "Thank you, Sammy."

"Gee," said the boy in his squeaky voice. "No one ever called me Sammy before. Just Samson. Because my adopted father wanted me to be as big as Glorious Leader and as bright as a professor."

"Well, to me you're a *Sammy*," said Kate.

"I sure did like your pie, Miss Kate," said Samson, trying to return the compliment and not quite knowing how. "Even if it was chicken."

H.T. looked steadily at the boy. His amber eyes fairly glowed. "Bless my father's sticky tongue," he said. "No one could call you chicken. You have to be brave to take such a chance as this."

"Chance? Brave?" asked the boy. It had not occurred to him that he was doing something dangerous. His voice quavered. "I never thought *I* could be brave. Take chances. I mean, the others always laughed at me."

Kate smiled again. In the dark her teeth glowed like a comfortable fire. "Don't let them get you down, Sammy. Good is always harder to do than evil. And lots of times it's more dangerous, too."

By this time Samson had gotten Kate untied and was turning to undo H.T. while Kate rubbed her wrists. "Gee, Mr. Toad, your arms are all slippery. No offense meant."

"Happens when I get annoyed," said H.T. pleasantly. "Like sweat. Doesn't smell though. Doesn't bother me any. But it sure can confound my enemies."

"Your friends, too." said Samson. "I can't get your ropes undone."

"Why don't you let me help?" thundered a voice as a bright spot of light stabbed at them from above. It was Glorious Leader, his bushy moustache quivering with rage. *"Professor,* come and see what your precious son has done."

There was a scrabbling as the Professor climbed down from Kate's cot and paddled into the room. "You ingrate! You . . ." he struggled furiously to find bad enough words, but no words came. Then they came in a torrent of evil: "I should have left you where I found you. I should never have stolen you from the doorstep of the foundling home. I should have let you grow up like any other normally stupid boy instead of wasting my time and money on trying to instill ideas of power and greatness into your thick skull. I should have known better than to try and make something of you."

"What shall we do with him?" asked Glorious Leader.

"Tie him up with the others," said the Professor. "I never did like the brat. And set a guard." With that, he went back to the cot and fell asleep.

Morning crept cold and quickly under the doorsill and around the curtains. The four prisoners had spent a miserable, cramped night awaiting their fate.

The Professor had taken an alarm clock to bed with him and its bell roused all the sleepers at once.

Since there were no more pies left to be eaten, the Devil's Dozen made some foul-smelling coffee and then set about their tasks. They got into their red suspenders, painted the stolen pickup truck red and

black and printed SECUNDO FIER DEPT on it, attached the schoolhouse bell to the cab, and looped the garden hose around the ladder. Several of the gang clapped toy fire chief hats on their heads. The spotted dog refused to ride on the running board and they finally had to put him in the front seat next to Glorious Leader, who was to drive.

Then, laughing and shouting, the Devil's Dozen lifted up Mac, H.T., Kate, and Samson, whose hands had been tied in front with his own red suspenders, and deposited them in Mac's truck. Samson was in the middle and he was quite squeezed between Kate's bulk and Mac. H.T. sat on his lap.

"Maybe you'll get warts!" shouted Creep joyfully to Samson.

The Professor, when he finished sawing apart the brake connection, leaped onto Creep's back and rode piggyback to the window of the truck. He leaned over Mac and said to H.T.:

> *"The ungainly toad*
> *That crawls from his secure abode*
> *Within the mossy garden wall*
> *Deserves to fall."*

"So you're a poet, too," said Mac.

"Just a few lines borrowed from the greatest poet of them all—Shakespeare," said the Professor with an evil smile. "And a fine epitaph, too, even if I had to make up the last line myself."

46

Then he turned to the rest of the gang. "Get this truck into position and then you all climb into the fire truck and coast to the bottom of the hill. At exactly nine o'clock I'll push this one over the rise. Then I'll race to Kate's diner and wait. You get in to the bank, get the money, and get out. We'll meet back here on the double."

The Devil's Dozen pushed the big truck to the top of the hill. Then, laughing and shouting, they climbed onto their newly painted fire truck and rolled away to the bottom of the hill where they parked, inconspicuously, in an alley around the corner from the bank.

At exactly nine o'clock, the Professor walked to the back of the big INFLAMMABLE truck and gave it a push. It crested the top of the hill and started to roll slowly, almost reluctantly, down the steep hill that ended at the bank.

The Professor began to laugh. "Bye-bye," he called. "Have a bang-up trip!" Then he skipped back to the diner and slammed the door, for he hated loud noises.

As the truck started down the hill, Kate groaned. "I knew from the moment I heard the Professor saying 'prehensile' that there was bound to be trouble."

Samson began to cry. He didn't want to—he wanted to be brave. But his chin started to wobble, and suddenly the tears came.

H.T. seemed ready to comfort the boy or at least say something, but Mac cut them all off short by starting to sing:

"Oh the joy of the open road,
In a truck that they think will explode,
Through the dawn and the dark and the dawn
Riding astraddle and also sidesaddle a traveling
    bomb.
Feet are all tied and likewise our hands,
Still with our mouths we can make plans
So we can stop before we explode
And spatter the road with a Kate, Mac, and Sam and
    occasional Toad!"

48

"**O**h for goodness' sake," said Kate, "how can you sing at a time like this?"

"I can *always* find time to sing," said Mac.

"Well," snuffled Samson, "I like it. I think if we sing it together, we won't be so afraid."

But H.T., who had been deep in thought, suddenly gave a joyful "Hrrrumph! We can use our mouths for more than just making plans, Mac. 'Prehensile,' eh? I'll show him!"

With that, H.T. turned to Samson and stuck out his tongue, that wonderful long, sticky, ingeniously wrought tongue that was fastened to the front of his mouth; that tongue—so unlike a human's—that was limber with years of catching bugs on the fly. Deftly

49

H.T. inserted his tongue between Samson's bound wrists and flicked up the catch on the suspenders that tied them. Then he flicked apart the knots. In less than a minute, Samson was free.

"Ugh!" said H.T. "Not half so tasty as flies."

"Never mind wasting your tongue on talk," said Mac. "Lick away!"

In the few seconds it took to undo Mac's bonds and for Samson to free Kate, Mac had completed a new song. "'For Hero Toad,'" he announced and opened his mouth to sing.

"Forget it," said H.T. "Just jump."

Mac opened his door and Kate opened hers. The toad and the truck driver leaped out the driver's side. Kate and the boy fell out of the other, rolling over one another. The truck continued down the hill, picking up speed as it headed toward its confrontation with the First National Bank of Secundo.

Mac fell to the ground with a loud crunch. His gold tooth was loosened in the fall and when H.T. rolled over him, it became stuck in the top of the toad's head.

"And I thought the jewel in the toad's head was an old wives' tale," said Mac with a laugh. And H.T. had to join him, even though it hurt.

As Kate hit the ground, a terrible thing happened. A button on her left hip, where she landed first, was torn almost loose from its moorings. And when she stood up and started up the hill toward the Grate, the

button could stand the strain no longer. It popped
loose from the last thin thread that held it to the
dress, with a loud *ping*. As it went, it seemed to set
off a chain reaction, and one after another, the hundreds of buttons on Kate's dress started to jiggle,

tense, strain, and pop, wildly *pinging* out. All the buttons on the front went first, straight toward the diner. And a good twenty-five or so hit the front door which was well within firing range. They *pinged* and *twanged* against the metal trolley-car door like a hail of machine gun bullets.

"Turn around, Kate, turn around," cried H.T. "Give it to him with both barrels!"

Kate, bewildered, did as she was told. And her back buttons pounded into the door as well.

Slowly, as the rain of buttons ended, the door of the diner was pushed open. A large white square flag, later identified as one of Kate's napkins, came fluttering into view.

"Don't shoot . . . please don't shoot anymore," came the Professor's weak whine. "I know when I'm surrounded. I give up." He stepped out, blinking, into the sunshine with his hands over his head.

By the time the Professor realized it was not the police but H.T., Mac, Kate, and his ex-adopted son Sammy, they had grabbed him anyway and tied him with the napkin. Sammy ran in to call the police. Just as Mac was putting the finishing touches on the knot, an enormous BAAAALLOOOOOM came from over the hill.

"You're too late!" rejoiced the Professor. "Before the police can come, my gang will be back with the money. And the police will be too busy battling the fire to look for us. Aha! You lose. Evil always conquers. Crime always pays!" And he hobbled away from his captors and raced to the top of the hill to look down at his wonderful fire.

Mac and H.T. and Kate ran after him.

But when they all peered down the hill, instead of a fire, they saw the truck, lodged in the front of the bank, spewing thousands upon thousands of colorful bits into the air and onto the sidewalks.

"Marbles," said Mac. "I've lost all my marbles!"

"*He's* lost *his* marbles," moaned the Professor. "I think I've lost mine."

And as they watched, the fake fire truck that had been waiting for the sound of the crash came careering around the corner on two wheels. The spotted dog, who had finally been coaxed onto the running board with a bit of leftover chicken pie, was thrown clear of the truck. He landed on the sidewalk with a yelp and raced all the way back to the kennel from which he had been stolen.

The twelve members of the Devil's Dozen leaped from the fire truck, the gold clasps of their red suspenders gleaming in the sun. They were moving so quickly that they never noticed that there wasn't any fire.

As each member of the gang jumped to the ground, he slipped on the dozens and dozens of marbles that were cascading from the demolished truck. One by

one, the hoodlums rolled down the marble pathway, which ended farther down the hill from the bank, at right angles to the route the truck had taken.

And the marble pathway ended right in front of the Secundo Police Station.

As the gang members piled up one at a time by

their front steps, the police, alerted by Sammy's call, picked them up and put them each in separate cells, even the twins Bobordick, who had never been parted before.

It was the neatest, cleanest, easiest arrest the Secundo police had ever made.

Hobo Toad, Great Kate, Mac, and Sammy were delighted.

"Evil spelled backwards may be *live*," shouted Sammy down the hill after his ex-adopted father who was departing in the police wagon, "but turned about a bit, it is also *vile*!"

Kate put her arm around Sammy. "Would you like some more chicken pie?" she said. "You look a little hungry."

"I think it's time for the Professor to eat pie, too," said H.T. to Great Kate, whose dress now hung limp and tentlike and buttonless on her ample figure.

"What do you mean?" asked Kate. "What kind of pie?"

"Why, humble pie, of course," said H.T. with a smile.

And they all laughed. Except—naturally—the Professor.

mac and H.T. had to stay in Secundo, of course. There was to be a grand celebration. Newspaper reporters came from all over to interview the Hero Toad, and after-dinner speeches were to be given by the mayor of Secundo, the police chief, and the head of the ladies' auxiliary. The president of the Greater Boston Marble Company came down for the medal-awarding ceremony and he gave a talk that began, "Marbles, my friends, have a history of social involvement that dates back to the days when marbles were buried with their owners in the great pyramids of Egypt."

Secundo had a grand parade in which the best

floats depicting the Great Event were awarded ribbons. H.T.'s favorite was the one which had the demolished truck spewing small round colored candies to the crowd. Kate was crowned Queen of the Fair and she rode on a float constructed entirely of pies.

Sam was made an honorary fire marshal, given monogrammed red suspenders, and officially adopted by Kate.

H.T. was given a silver-plated acorn pipe and the keys to the city of Secundo.

And Mac had his poem "For Hero Toad" privately printed by the First National Bank of Secundo in a special booklet. He even got to read it on a local TV show.

FOR HERO TOAD

Now toads aren't so handsome they'd make you look twice,
But despite their appearance they're worth any price.
And you'd be very dumb
To ignore the big thumb
Of a hitchhiking toad—and that's sure my advice.

My friend is a toad, and I'm sure you'll agree
They're the best folks to ride with—occasionally—
And the very best time
Is when there's been a crime
And you don't want the hoodlums to get off scot-free.

Some folks look at toads with disgust and disdain.
They point to some warts and they cry and complain.
But most folks, you see,
With McNeill will agree
That if Toad has a jewel in his head it's his brain!

And of course everyone in Secundo and the sur-
rounding towns as well—not to mention representa-
tives from *Time, Newsweek,* and the underground
press—attended the trial of the Professor and his
twelve sidekicks. The hoodlums were given twenty
years apiece for robbery, assault, malicious damage,
and impersonating fire chiefs. The Professor was
found not guilty on this last count since he did not
even have a pair of red suspenders, but he was charged

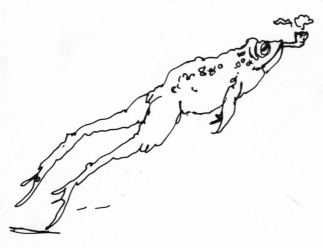

with cruelty to a child, and all the mothers in
Secundo, led by Kate, booed when he stood up and
tried to plead "Not Guilty."

Mac got to write a first-person account for *Life*

60

magazine, and *Women's Wear Daily* described the Great Kate Button Dress which became all the rage and replaced miniskirts for a year.

All in all, it was two weeks and three days before Mac and H.T.—which now stood officially for Hero Toad as well as Hopalong Toad, having been written in on his birth certificate and passport in indelible ink by the mayor and stamped with the Secundo town seal—could start again for Okefenokee. Mac, of course, had a new truck filled with marbles which had been driven down by the president of the company himself. Instead of INFLAMMABLE, this one said THE GREATER BOSTON MARBLE COMPANY . . . *If you've lost your marbles, we'll replace them* . . . THE MARBLES THAT MAKE BANKS SAFE.

"That was a lot of fun," said Mac as they started out of Secundo at last. "But I sure am glad to be back on the road."

"Yes," said H.T., smoke from his new silver-plated pipe wreathing his head. "The swamp will certainly seem quiet after Secundo." And he smiled a contented toad smile, for toads are really quiet, retiring sorts.

And the two went on for a while, as friends will, sharing a companionable silence. And when, spontaneously, they burst into the road song together at the same time, they sang it joyously and in a rhythm that matched the rolling sound of the southbound wheels of the truck.

61

"Oh, the joy of the open road,
Traveling with an occasional toad.
Through the dawn and the dark and the dawn,
Traveling on and on and on and on and on.
Wheeling on down the dusty highway,
Picking up somebody going my way.
Oh, there's no joy like a big diesel load
But the joy, joy, joy of the open road."

ABOUT THE AUTHOR

JANE YOLEN is a young author with an astonishing number of books to her credit. Among these are *World on a String, Greyling, The Wizard of Washington Square,* and *The Emperor and the Kite,* which was the runner-up for the Caldecott Award in 1968. After her graduation from Smith College, Jane Yolen worked for several years as a children's book editor. Now married to David W. Stemple, a vice president in charge of research at a computer company, she has two young children and lives in Bolton, Massachusetts.

ABOUT THE ILLUSTRATOR

EMILY McCULLY went to Pembroke College, then got her master's degree in art history from Columbia University. Now married and the mother of a young son, she lives in Swarthmore, Pennsylvania, where her husband teaches Renaissance history. A free-lance illustrator of children's books, she has won a gold medal from the Philadelphia Art Directors' Club, and also designed the Children's Book Week poster for 1969.